THE BOY
WHO FELL IN LOVE
WITH A
WOLF GIRL

To order additional copies of this book, contact:
Xlibris
1-888-795-4274
www.Xlibris.com
Orders@Xlibris.com

ISBN: Softcover   978-1-7960-9809-9
         EBook   978-1-7960-9808-2

Print information available on the last page

Rev. date: 04/17/2020

THE BOY
WHO FELL IN LOVE
WITH A
WOLF GIRL

ANNABELLA ROSE

The girl was walking in the woods and she hears something, it's her childhood wolves in the woods.

But then she saw the angel wolf she is so shocked that she almost started to cry and the wolves licked her face and she cried more and more and she asked the wolves, "Would you like to go with me of my journey?"

So the wolves followed and they went to wolf town.

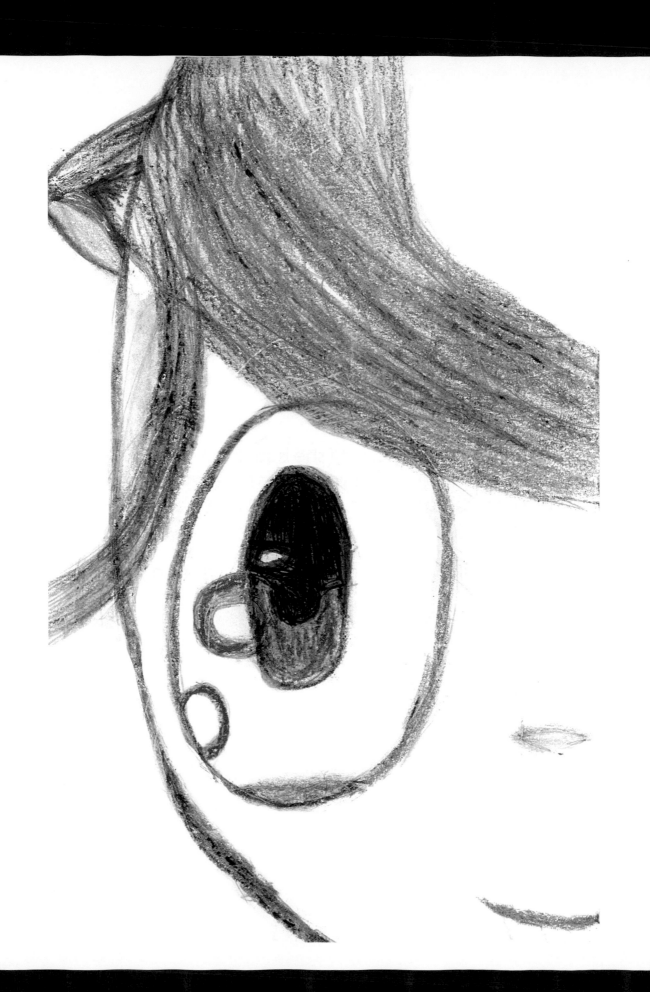

She saw a boy at the wolf town

She looked at the boy in his eyes., he looked familiar.

And it was funny so fast she ran and the boy ran after.

He was amazed by her wolf pack.

And that's where they met. She is walking and she sees a town and she went to eat something and she hoped to make new friends.

They see the town she started to walk in wolf town with the boy.

The wolves smelled something.

They then started to run up to the town.

The people stared they have never seen a wolf girl with a wolf pack, "yes I am a wolf girl I was lost in the woods." said to the boy in wolf town.

The boy held her hand and he said, "Nice to meet you".

The boy said you look familiar the wolf girl lily said, "I was left in the woods by my evil mother the wolves took care of me we played and chased each other".

They talked about the boy's family. The girl was quiet for a minute the boy said, "What's wrong?" lily said, "nothing." and they walked toward the boy's castle.

He was a prince of wolf town.

As lily and the boy walked up to the castle all she can think was her evil mother.

No one knows that lily's dad died in a war and lily was thrown away in the woods so her mom could be Queen. Lily said, "I am scared, I have been in the wood and I am dirty with my wolf pack. What if they don't like us?

"It's ok you are going to be fine. I will keep you safe." said the boy prince.

So they walk up to the palace but then she saw her evil mother.

The king was concerned. He didn't know what was going on. He asked, his son who is this girl as the king an evil Queen stood there looking mad and thinking curious. Before she could answer the evil Queen had her taken to get cleaned up. The evil Queen said – "I know your lily how did you survive?", as she bathed her. "The wolves took care of me.", said lily, lily asked, "why did you leave me in the woods?" The evil Queen said, "I wanted to be queen and your father died in the war." Lilly begged to get back to her wolf pack.

The evil mother said, "We will eat dinner and you won't say a word that I left you in the woods". Lily cried.

As they came down for dinner

Lily saw her wolf pack all cleaned up and boy prince standing there with the king. The evil step mother said to the prince and lily go play till we call for dinner.

Lily and the boy played with the wolf pack, "what a great palace you have".

Lily stopped and said to the boy prince. "I have to tell you a secret promise you won't tell".

The boy Prince came closer as the wolf pack circled the wolf girl Lilly, she began to speak but the evil mother calls them for dinner.

The king and the prince come out to get them and the evil mother says, "Let me speak to lily before dinner you guys run along will be in a minute". Lily began to shiver, the wolf pack began to snarl and growl. Lily commands the wolf pack to her side, the king and the prince. As they walked away towards the castle

The evil mother says, "I will put you in the dungeon if you ever tell I left you in the woods to be queen", with an evil look in her eyes. She pushes lily to the ground and says, "no one will take a way my crown" The wolf pack begins to growl at the queen. Lily cries and the wolf pack attacked the queen. Lily screamed, "NO" to the wolf pack as the prince and king come running out from hearing the noise.

The queen screams, "put them in the dungeon with her wolf pack"

Lily says, "NO MOTHER NO MOTHER".

The king says, "Mother? How is this possible?" Then lily cried and said, "She left me in the woods to die after my father died in the war so she could be queen." The king was in disbelief. He said to the queen staring confused, "Is this true my queen?

The evil mother attacked lily and she began to choke her. The wolf pack pounced on the queen and began to eat her to pieces as lily cried, the boy prince screamed and the king starred helplessly the wolf pack had ate the queen. Lily and her pack ran off back to the woods

The boy prince and the king were in shock how could this be so he sent a few of his army men to go and find Lily. The prince said, "I must go too and find Lily, I will never go with your army". The king agreed and off they went far off in the woods to find lily and her wolf pack.

For days and days they searched for Lilly but could not find her and no sign or track of lily's wolf pack.

As the boy laid next to the fire. Tired he sobbed and feared he might never see Lilly again, a sister he never knew.

Then he heard a crunch of leaves in the distance as if someone was there.

It was

It was Lilly and her wolf pack.

How happy the boy was when he found Lilly, his sister. "Lilly I been looking for you I'm so happy I found you. Please come back to the palace with me, we are family and your wolf pack will be honored."

As a tear fell down on Lilly's face, she hugged the boy prince her brother.

She said, "And the evil mother?"

"She is dead". Says the boy prince.

"The king is waiting for us. He wants to hear your story, Lilly and make you a princess and your wolf pack the pride of wolf town. We will celebrate your return"

Lilly, her wolf pack, the boy prince and the army that the king sent was making their journey back from wolf town to their palace. One of the horse man sound off a horn as they approached the palace.

The town was cheering as roses are thrown, "it's a celebration" as they have returned.

Printed in the United States
by Baker & Taylor Publisher Services